For Max and Sophia

Also by Sophie Kinsella

Fairy Mom and Me
Fairy Mom and Me #2: Fairy in Waiting
Fairy Mom and Me #3: Fairy Unicorn Wishes

THE SHOPAHOLIC SERIES

Confessions of a Shopaholic
Shopaholic Takes Manhattan
Shopaholic Ties the Knot
Shopaholic & Sister
Shopaholic & Baby
Mini Shopaholic
Shopaholic to the Stars
Shopaholic to the Rescue
Christmas Shopaholic

OTHER NOVELS

I Owe You One
Surprise Me
My (Not So) Perfect Life
Finding Audrey
Wedding Night
I've Got Your Number
Twenties Girl
Remember Me?
The Undomestic Goddess
Can You Keep a Secret?

SOPHIE KINSELLA

Fairy Mermaid Magic

illustrated by
Marta Kissi

A Yearling Book

Text copyright © 2020 by Sophie Kinsella
Cover art and interior illustrations copyright © 2020 by Marta Kissi

All rights reserved. Published in the United States by Yearling, an imprint of
Random House Children's Books, a division of Penguin Random House LLC,
New York. Originally published in hardcover in the United States by Delacorte Press,
an imprint of Random House Children's Books, New York, in 2020.

Yearling and the jumping horse design are
registered trademarks of Penguin Random House LLC.

Visit us on the Web! rhcbooks.com

Educators and librarians, for a variety of teaching tools,
visit us at RHTeachersLibrarians.com

Library of Congress Cataloging-in-Publication Data is available upon request.
ISBN 978-0-593-12052-1 (trade) — ISBN 978-0-593-12053-8 (ebook)
ISBN 978-0-593-12054-5 (pbk.)

Printed in the United States of America
10 9 8 7 6 5 4 3 2 1
First Yearling Edition 2021

Random House Children's Books supports the First Amendment
and celebrates the right to read.

Contents

Meet Fairy Mom and Me

Hi. My name is Ella Brook and I live
in a town called Cherrywood with my mom,
my dad and my baby brother, Ollie.

My mom looks normal, just like any
other mom . . . but she's not. Because she can
turn into a fairy. All she has to do is stamp
her feet three times, clap her hands, wiggle
her bottom and say, "Marshmallow," . . .
and POOF! She's Fairy Mom. Then if
she says, "Toffee apple," she's just Mom
again.

All the girls in my family turn into fairies when they grow up. My Aunty Jo and Granny did. They can all fly and turn invisible and do real magic. Mom and Aunty Jo also have a really cool wand called a Computawand V5. The wand has magic powers, a computer screen, Fairy Apps, Fairy Mail and Fairy Games!

The problem is that Mom is still not very good at doing magic spells, even though she works really hard at her lessons on FairyTube with her Fairy Tutor, Fairy Fenella. But one day she's going to get everything right.

When I'm grown up, I'll be a fairy like her! Mom calls me her Fairy in Waiting. I'll

have big sparkly wings and my own beautiful shiny crown, and I'll be able to do magic just like Mom.

Being a Fairy in Waiting is a big secret. I'm not allowed to tell anyone, not even my best friends, Tom and Lenka. And I definitely can't tell my Not-Best Friend, Zoe. She is the meanest girl ever and she lives next door. Sometimes I think she might find out about Mom being a fairy.

But she hasn't yet.

And there are lots of things I like besides magic. I love drawing and making things. I love sparkles and cupcakes. I *especially* love unicorns and mermaids. I sometimes wish Mom could do a magic spell and turn me into a mermaid. If I was a grown-up fairy, that's what I would do. But she always says, "We'll see, Ella."

MERMAIDERIDOO!

The Great Whale Rescue

One day we went to the seaside. There was a café by the beach and we bought some cakes for a snack.

"What a lovely baby!" said the café lady. "May I hold him?" She took Ollie and he smiled at her. "Aren't you lovely!" she said to him. "What's your name?"

"Weezi-weezi-weezi!" he said, and splatted his cake in her face. She was covered in creamy icing.

"Ollie!" said Dad, and he grabbed Ollie back. "I'm so sorry!"

"Don't worry!" said the lady, wiping icing from her eyes. "He didn't know what he was doing, bless him."

Grown-ups always think Ollie doesn't know what he's doing. I think he knows exactly what he's doing.

* * *

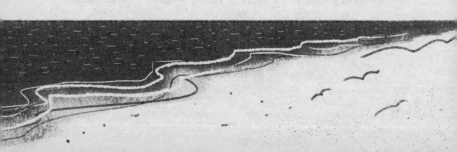

We left the café before Ollie could splat anything else, and went down to the beach. Dad carried Ollie on his shoulders and I skipped along on the pebbles.

Dad showed me how to skip rocks on the water. We made sandcastles and Ollie tried to eat the sand. Then Mom said she wanted

to stretch her legs and go on a long walk. Ollie is not very good at going on long walks, because he always sits down and cries. So Dad said he would look after Ollie while Mom and I explored.

"Make sure you find some buried treasure!" he said.

"We will!" said Mom. "Ready, Captain Ella?"

We walked along the beach to a little cliff with lots of rocks at the bottom of it. We couldn't see past the rocks, so we guessed what we would find on the other side of them. I guessed an octopus in a rock pool. Mom guessed a pirate ship.

We climbed around the rocks—then stopped in astonishment. There was a whale on the beach. An actual real-life whale! It was enormous and it had shiny gray skin.

I was really excited, but Mom wasn't. She blew out hard and said, "I didn't guess *that*." Then she said, "Whales aren't supposed to be on the beach, Ella. They belong in the water. That whale is in trouble. It's stuck."

There were lots of people standing around the whale. Some of them were sloshing water on it. Some of them were on their phones. Everyone looked worried.

When we got closer, Mom asked a man if we could help.

The man told us, "We need to get this whale out to sea." He explained that once the tide came in, they would float the whale back into the water. They hoped it would find its way home.

The whale looked very sad. It was thrashing its tail back and forth as if it was trying to get unstuck from the beach. I wished I could speak whale language and tell it we were going to help it. Then I had an idea.

"Mom!" I said. "Can you use a magic spell and speak

to the whale? You could explain that we're
going to help it."

"Yes!" said Mom. "That's a very good
idea, Ella."

Mom went behind a big rock where no

one could see her. She stamped her feet three times, clapped her hands, wiggled her bottom and said, "Marshmallow," . . . and POOF! She was a fairy. She pointed at herself, pressed a code on her Computawand—*bleep-bleep-bloop*—and said, "Inviseridoo!" Then no one could see her—except me, because I'm a Fairy in Waiting.

Then she pressed another code—
bleep-bleep-bloop—and said, "Speakeridoo!
Whaleridoo! Come on, Ella. Now I can talk to
the whale."

Mom carefully made her way through all
the people to the whale's head and whispered
to it. After a moment the whale stopped
thrashing its tail. It seemed to be listening
quietly. It even made some whale sounds
back. I felt very proud of Mom.

A few minutes later, Mom came back to
me and said, "The whale is very young. He
got lost and needs to find his way back to his
mother."

I felt very sorry for the whale. I know how

scary it is to lose your mom, because I once lost Mom in a big store. Since then I always hold her hand really tightly. But whales don't have hands.

"Do you know where his mother is?" I asked Mom.

"No. But I know who might be able to help," she said.

"Who?"

Mom bit her lip and said, "I really ought to take you back to Dad. . . ."

At once I knew Mom was going to do something exciting.

"Wait," I said quickly. "Please take me too. How will I learn to be a good fairy

if I don't come with you and help?"

Mom laughed. "Ella, you always have a good answer. All right, Fairy in Waiting— you can come. We're going to fly, so I'll need to make you invisible, and you'll need to hold my hand tight."

"I will!" I said. "I promise!"

I took Mom's hand and squeezed as tightly as I could. She pressed two codes on her Computawand—*bleep-bleep-bloop . . . bleep-bleep-bloop*—and said, "Inviseridoo! Flyeridoo!"

The next moment we were both invisible and flying over the sea. The air was cold and salty. I could see little white waves far below

us. Then I saw some rocks right in the middle of the sea. We started flying down toward them. I could see a glimmer of silver. It was moving, and I wondered if we were going to meet some seals.

As we got closer, my mouth dropped open. Having a fairy for a mom means lots of surprises. But this was the biggest surprise *ever*.

Sitting on the rocks were two mermaids. They had long silver fish tails and long dark hair—and they didn't look happy to see us.

"Stay very quiet, Ella," Mom said as we landed gently on the rocks. "Mermaids are

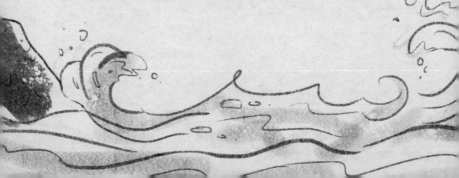

very scared of humans, and they're nervous around fairies too, even though we are friends."

I had never seen real mermaids before. We sat on the rocks and Mom talked in a low voice in a language I couldn't understand. Gradually the mermaids looked less worried. They all nodded at each other.

"I've asked the mermaids to guide the whale back to his mother," said Mom. "I'll make them invisible too, so they'll be safe."

One of the mermaids smiled at me and I waved at her. Her eyes were sea-green and there was seaweed woven through her hair.

I thought she was beautiful.

"Hello," I said, even though I didn't know if she could understand me.

She gave me a little pink stone carved with patterns, and I said, "Thank you!" I put it safely in my pocket.

Then Mom stood up. "We must get back to the whale," she said. "We could fly . . . or shall we swim?" Her eyes twinkled.

I gasped. "Can we be mermaids too?" I said, and Mom laughed.

"Not real mermaids. But we can have mermaid tails for a little bit. Although it's even *more* important that you stay with me, Ella," she added. "You don't want

to get lost like the whale."

She pressed a code on her Computa-wand—*bleep-bleep-bloop*—pointed it at the mermaids and said, "Inviseridoo!" Then she pressed another code, pointed it at us and said, "Mermaideridoo!"

At once I had the strangest feeling. My
legs seemed to grow together. They felt cool
and strong and slippery. I looked down and
couldn't believe it—I had a mermaid tail!

We all slipped into the water. It
didn't feel cold—it felt soft. It didn't

sting my eyes like normal, and when I went underwater, I realized I could breathe, even though I didn't have a snorkel! Fairy Mom sometimes gets her spells wrong—but today she had gotten all her magic right! Just when we needed it most.

"Ready?" Mom asked, and she grabbed my hand tight. Then—whoosh! We were zooming through the water. It felt like flying, not swimming.

As we went, I saw blue and yellow fish and a turtle and an octopus. I wished we could be mermaids forever, but before long we were back at the beach. We could see Dad standing on the sand with all the people, holding Ollie in his arms.

Mom swam with me to the shallow water. She did another spell so everyone could see me again and said, "Go find Dad, Ella. Tell him what's happened. I will stay with the whale and the mermaids."

Just then a man on the beach saw me and his eyes went very wide. "Little girl!" he shouted. "What are you doing? Get out at once! No one is allowed in the water! You might upset the whale!"

Everyone was staring at me, but I didn't know what to do. I couldn't get out because I didn't have any legs, only a mermaid tail.

"Mom!" I yelled. "I haven't got any legs!"

"Oh," she said. "Oops. Let's change you back." She pressed a code on her Computawand, then said, "Normeridoo!"

Right away I felt my feet again and started paddling to shore. I missed my mermaid tail, but at least I still had my pink stone from the friendly mermaid.

"Little girl!" said the man again. "Are you by yourself?"

"She's with me!" Dad hurried forward. "Ella, sweetheart, let's get you dry."

I came out of the sea and Dad wrapped me in a towel. "What's your mother doing?" he asked in a low voice.

"Saving the whale," I whispered back. "With the mermaids."

"Ah," said Dad. "I imagined it was something like that."

* * *

While everyone was waiting for the tide to come in, Dad looked around the beach. It was covered with litter. There were cans and old potato chip bags and even a broken tent. "We can't save the whale, Ella," he said. "But we can still be useful."

He stood on a high rock, with Ollie in his arms. He said, "Attention, everybody! There are lots of special experts helping the whale. The rest of us can be useful in another way. We can clear this beach so that it is beautiful and clean again. If you want to help, then cheer."

All the people cheered really loudly! I felt so proud of Dad. He isn't magic like Mom, but he is amazing in different ways.

We all started collecting litter. Even Ollie

helped. We gathered it into bags and put them at the top of the beach to be sorted out.

After a while the sea started to come up the beach. The waves were getting closer and closer.

"Look!" said Dad. "The tide is coming in. It's time for the whale to float back out to sea."

We went up the steps onto the cliff so we would be safe. After a long time the tide was high enough and the whale slowly began to move through the water. I could see Mom and the mermaids swimming at his side, although no one else could.

Everyone started cheering. "The whale

is saved!" cried a lady with curly hair. "It's a miracle!"

I knew it wasn't a miracle—it was Mom and the mermaids. But I couldn't say that. I just looked at Dad and we smiled at each other.

When the whale had swum right out to sea, the man in charge of the rescue made a speech. He thanked everyone for their help and he said he hoped the whale would find his way home. Then he said, "And a special thank-you to Mr. Brook for organizing the litter cleanup. The beach has never looked so good!"

As everyone was clapping, Mom crept up

to join us. She wasn't a fairy anymore. Her hair was wet, but she looked very pleased. "The whale has found his mother," she said quietly, and I was so happy I gave her a hug.

Then the lady with curly hair said to me, "Your father is a star. He has made the world a better place."

I wanted to tell the lady that Mom was a star too, and that she had saved the whale. But I knew I couldn't. So I just smiled and nodded and said, "I know."

* * *

On the way home I drew some pictures in my book. I drew the whale. I drew the mermaids. I drew Dad standing on the rock and all the people cheering.

I thought how proud I was of both my mom and dad. I thought about how they had made the world a better place. And I hoped that one day I would make the world a better place too.

VOLCANERIDOO!

Who Says Science and Magic Don't Mix?

One day after school, I was doing my science project at home. Mom was helping me color in my poster about volcanoes, but she kept going outside the lines.

"Mom," I said, "Miss Amy likes us to stay *inside* the lines."

"Sorry, Ella," Mom said. Then she looked

at her watch. "Coloring takes a long time, doesn't it? How about we speed this up?"

I knew she meant she was going to do a magic spell.

"I don't mind doing the coloring," I said quickly, because sometimes when Mom tries to speed things up with magic, it doesn't exactly work out. But Mom didn't listen. She stamped her feet three times, clapped her hands, wiggled her bottom and said, "Marshmallow," and POOF! She was a fairy.

She got her phone from her bag and I watched as it came alive and turned into a Computawand. She pressed a code—*bleep-*

bleep-bloop—then pointed the wand at the markers on the table and said, "Coloridoo!"

The markers flew up from the table and started coloring my poster all by themselves! They colored very fast and very neatly. I stared at them with wide eyes, wishing I could color like that.

"There!" said Mom, looking pleased. "It just goes to show you—"

Then she stopped. She was looking over my shoulder, and her face was kind of frozen. I turned around and gasped.

Behind us, all the other markers from my pencil case had flown up and started coloring too. They were coloring the kitchen cabinets, the ceiling, the lampshade . . . everything!

A blue pen was coloring the bananas in the fruit bowl. A red pen was coloring Ollie's face while he laughed and said, "Weezi-weezi-weezi!"

Quickly Mom pressed a different code—*bleep-bleep-bloop*—and shouted, "Stoperidoo!" The markers all fell down just as Dad came into the kitchen with Aunty Jo.

Dad and Aunty Jo looked at all the colorful kitchen cabinets.

"Interesting," said Dad. "Have you been redecorating?"

46

"No," said Mom, turning red. "I was helping Ella color her project. The markers got carried away."

"Tragic," said Aunty Jo. "*And* the dinner's burning."

"It's not burning!" said Mom, looking worried as she rushed over to the oven. "It's just . . . crispy."

"If you say so," said Aunty Jo. "Shall I give you a hand?"

While Dad and Mom got dinner out, I set the table and Aunty Jo turned into a

fairy. She cleared up all the coloring with a magic spell, and then made Ollie laugh with magic rainbow bubbles. Then both she and Mom went back to normal and we sat down to eat.

During dinner I told Aunty Jo about

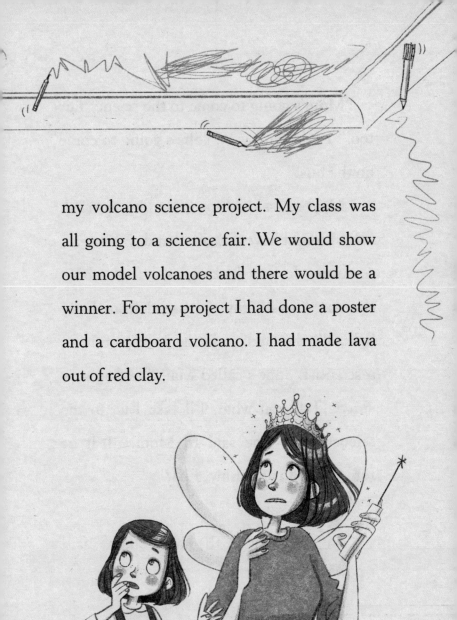

my volcano science project. My class was all going to a science fair. We would show our model volcanoes and there would be a winner. For my project I had done a poster and a cardboard volcano. I had made lava out of red clay.

"Mom's going to come to the science fair too!" I told Aunty Jo. "She's going to come on the bus!"

"Maybe," said Mom, sounding worried. "But I might have to work that day, Ella."

Aunty Jo was looking at a flyer about the fair. "That's my old friend from Fairy School!" she said, pointing to a picture of a scientist. "She's called Mai. She was very smart. Tell you what, I'll take Ella to the science fair," she said to Mom. "It'll be fun. What do you think, Ella?"

"Cool!" I said.

"But no magic at the science fair," said Mom to Aunty Jo.

"I know!" said Aunty Jo, rolling her eyes. "Of course!"

Mom and Dad looked at each other. Aunty Jo sometimes promises not to do magic but then does it anyway. Luckily, she is very good at magic. She has won lots of fairy prizes. Mom hasn't won any fairy prizes, but I know she will one day.

As I ate my ice cream, I was thinking hard.

In science our teacher said that gravity makes things go down. But the markers hadn't gone down—they'd gone up in the air.

"How do magic and science both work?" I asked.

"You'll learn that at Fairy School," said Mom. "When you're a big girl."

"I still don't understand how they both work," said Aunty Jo. "But Mai does. You can ask her."

＊ ＊ ＊

When I got on the bus to go to the science fair, my friends Tom and Lenka were already there. They had their model volcanoes too.

Lenka's was really good. It had red crinkly paper and twinkling lights.

My Not-Best-Friend Zoe was on the bus too, and her mother was giving out cookies.

"My mom is the best," Zoe was boasting. "Look at her cookies. No one else has cookies."

Aunty Jo looked at Zoe for a moment, then said, "Wait a minute, Ella. I've forgotten something."

She stepped off the bus, and a minute later she came back holding a plate of cookies. They were enormous, with candies all over them.

"You're not the only one with cookies,"

she said to Zoe with a nice smile. "Ella has cookies too."

"Look at those!" said Tom. "They're epic!"

"They're awesome!" said Lenka.

Everyone wanted one of Aunty Jo's cookies. No one was eating Zoe's mom's cookies.

"Aunty Jo!" I whispered. "Did you use magic?"

Aunty Jo just winked and passed me one. I knew Mom would be worried if she knew, but I couldn't help feeling happy as I saw everyone eating the amazing cookies.

Zoe wasn't pleased, though. She looked at me with small, angry eyes, and I knew she would try to get back at me somehow.

* * *

The science fair was held in a great big hall. We put our projects on a special table. Then we walked around looking at all the displays.

There were lots of tables where scientists were showing their experiments.

One scientist had a model of all the planets. Another one had some super-strong magnets that could make paper clips move without touching them.

"Cool!" said Tom as he watched. "It's just like magic!"

I looked at Aunty Jo and she smiled at me. Then she said, "Look, there's Mai!"

A woman was coming toward us. She had

short dark hair and a sweatshirt covered with numbers. She looked so much like a scientist that at first I couldn't believe she was a fairy too. But then I remembered that Mom and Aunty Jo don't look like fairies either. And I don't look much like a Fairy in Waiting.

Mai was very friendly. She showed us her display. It had light beams that turned into rainbows. Then she asked, "Are you interested in science, Ella?"

"Yes," I said. I looked around to make sure no one

would hear me, then added, "Science is like magic."

"It's a different kind of magic," said Mai, nodding. "Being a Fairy Scientist is wonderful. It's the most exciting kind of scientist you can be. Maybe one day you will be a Fairy Scientist."

I decided I would definitely be a Fairy Scientist when I grew up. And have a unicorn. Both.

"Let me see your project, Ella," said Mai, and we walked to the project table.

She looked at all the model volcanoes. But we couldn't see my volcano anywhere. I started to feel worried. I knew I had put it on the table.

"Where's my volcano?" I said. "I can't be in the competition if I don't have a volcano."

"Don't worry!" said Mai. "I'll ask the lady in charge if she's seen it."

As she was walking away, I noticed Zoe standing nearby, watching us. "Have you lost your project, Ella?" she said in a mean voice. "What a shame." Then she laughed her horrible laugh and ran off.

I felt sure she had something to do with my disappearing volcano. I looked at Aunty

Jo and I could tell she was thinking the same thing, because her face was all worried.

"I'll make you a new volcano," she said. "An even better volcano. I'll make sure you win the competition, Ella."

"Aunty Jo!" I said quickly. "Remember what Mom said!"

But she wasn't listening. Aunty Jo marched off behind a screen, and I guessed she was turning into a fairy. Suddenly I heard her say, "Volcaneridoo!"

She was doing magic!

A few moments later, she came back looking normal and holding a volcano model. I stared at it, astonished.

It was made out of painted cardboard, just like my volcano, but it had real flames bursting out of the top and it was making loud exploding noises.

Bang!
BOOM!
Sizzle!

"There!" said Aunty Jo, looking pleased. "*There's* a project for you."

I gasped. "Is that real fire?"

"It's Fairy Fire. Don't worry—it can't burn you. Isn't it great?" said Aunty Jo, looking

pleased with herself.

But a man walking past didn't think it looked great. When he spotted the volcano, he shouted, "Fire! Fire!" Then two children nearby started shouting, "Fire!" and soon there was a crowd of people around us, all shouting, "Fire! Help! Put it out!"

"It's *supposed* to be on fire!" said Aunty Jo, rolling her eyes. "It's a volcano! Didn't you learn that in science, any of you?"

"Aunty Jo," I begged, "can't you put the fire out?"

"But then you won't win the prize," she said. "Ooh, look, it's going to explode again."

The volcano made a massive noise—

—and flames leaped up to the ceiling. Some of the children started crying and some were laughing, and one boy shouted, "Again! Again!"

"Freezeridoo!" came a loud voice behind us, and I spun around to see Mai. She had turned into a fairy, with huge shimmery wings and a shiny metal crown, and she was holding a Computawand.

All the people at the fair had frozen like statues. No one could see or hear us.

"Jo!" said Mai Fairy. "What are you doing? This is a science fair, not a Fairy Fair."

"I know," said Aunty Jo, biting her lip. "I'm sorry. I just wanted Ella to have a great project. It's not fair. Ella worked very hard at her volcano, and I *know* Zoe did something to it."

Mai Fairy looked at me. And then she looked at Zoe, who was frozen nearby. Then she said, "Let's see what happened to your volcano, shall we, Ella?"

She pressed an extra-long code on her Computawand—*bleep-bleep-bleepity-bloop*—and said, "Trackeridoo!"

A beam of light came out of her Computawand. We followed it to a table at the side of the hall. The light beam was shining brightly on a trash can under the table—and in the can was my volcano.

I grabbed it out of the trash at once and petted it. "My volcano!"

I was so happy to see it again.

"And let's see how it got there," said Mai Fairy. She pressed another

really long code—*bleep-bleep-bleepity-bloop*—and another beam of light came out of her Computawand. This time it shone straight at Zoe.

"Oh dear," said Mai Fairy, looking sad. "Why would another girl want to put your volcano in the trash, Ella?"

"She was mad because Aunty Jo made magic cookies that were better than her mom's," I told Mai Fairy.

Mai Fairy gasped. "Jo! You used magic *twice* today? At a school?"

"I'm sorry!" said Aunty Jo again. "Sorry, Ella."

"But Zoe is always mean to me," I told Mai Fairy. "That's why she is my Not-Best Friend."

Mai Fairy thought about this for a moment. Then she smiled. "I will tell you something, Ella," she said. "Sometimes people are mean to me."

"No they're not," I said, because grown-ups aren't mean. Not mean like Zoe.

But Mai Fairy nodded. "Yes they are. They say mean things about my work. And there are lots of things I could do. I could do a magic spell on them and make their noses turn green. Or I could cry. Or I could give

up." She looked at me and said, "What do you think I do, Ella?"

I wanted to say, "You turn their noses green," but I knew that wasn't the right answer. "I don't know," I said, and Mai Fairy smiled.

"I remember that I am a strong fairy.

I say, 'Sorry, I'm too busy to listen to you right now.' And I just carry on with my work." Mai Fairy patted my hand. "Now, go and put your volcano on the table while your aunt and I use some Fairy Dust so none of the people here will remember what has happened," she said, smiling. Then she said, "Treacle tart!" and instantly she was normal again.

I put my model volcano carefully on the table while Aunty Jo and Mai sprinkled Fairy Dust all over the people at the fair. For about ten seconds everyone stayed completely still. They had sort of gone to sleep. Then . . .

"Go!" said Mai, and they all woke up.

As soon as Zoe saw me by the display table, she came running up. She stared at my volcano as though she couldn't believe her eyes.

"You found your volcano!" she said. "I don't understand. You *found* it."

"Yes," I said. "I did. Wasn't that lucky?"

* * *

When they gave prizes out for the volcanoes, I didn't win one. Neither did Zoe. But Lenka did!

I gave her a big hug and said, "Well done, Lenka!"

Then we were given sheets with pictures of volcanoes to color. I was coloring mine carefully when Zoe came up really close to me. She looked at me with her small, angry eyes.

"I bet you feel stupid now, Ella," she said. "You made all that fuss about your volcano, but you didn't win."

I looked at her for a moment. I thought about what Mai had said. I thought, *I am a strong Fairy in Waiting. And one day I will be a Fairy Scientist.*

Then I smiled at Zoe and said, "Sorry, Zoe. I'm too busy to listen to you right now." And I got on with my work.

POTTERIDOO!

Fairies Behaving Badly

It was Aunty Jo's birthday, and Mom and I were wrapping her present. Mom had bought her a new book called *Fairy Yoga*. We wrapped it in flowery paper. I thought it looked lovely, but Mom frowned.

"It doesn't look very special," she said.

"Jo's presents always look special."

I knew what she meant. On Mom's birthday Aunty Jo had given her a present wrapped with six different kinds of ribbon and a flower decoration.

Mom made a ribbon bow and tied it around the present, but it didn't look very good. It was floppy and messy. Mom pulled it tighter, trying to make it look better, but all she did was rip the wrapping paper. She sighed and pulled the paper off the book.

"Okay, that's it," she said. "I'm using magic."

"Or we could just try again," I said quickly—but Mom didn't hear me. She stamped her feet three times, clapped her hands, wiggled her bottom and said, "Marshmallow," . . . and POOF! She was a fairy. She pointed at the book, pressed a code on her Computawand—*bleep-bleep-bloop*—and said, "Wrapperidoo!"

At once the book was covered in shiny silver paper, with gold ribbon and a huge gold pom-pom. It looked *amazing*.

"There!" Mom said. "Isn't that fantastic?"

Then, in front of my eyes, the TV was wrapped up. One minute it was a normal TV. The next it was wrapped up in shiny orange paper, with blue ribbon and a big bow.

"Mom," I said, "look at the—" Then I stopped and gasped, because now the sofa was wrapped up too. It was covered in red-and-white stripy paper, with a tinsel bow. "Mom!" I said. "Everything's being wrapped up!"

"Oops," said Mom, looking astonished. "I don't know how *that* happened. Where did I put my Computawand?"

While Mom looked around for her Computawand, the table was suddenly wrapped up in pink polka-dotted paper, with three different-colored ribbons. Then the lamp was covered in sparkly tissue paper and a velvet flower decoration.

I loved everything being wrapped up. It looked as if the room was filled with presents. In fact, it felt like Christmas!

"Here it is!" Mom said as she found her Computawand under some wrapping paper. She quickly pressed a code—*bleep-bleep-bloop*—and said, "Stoperidoo!"

We waited breathlessly for a little while, but nothing else got wrapped up.

Just then Dad came into the room with Ollie. "What on *earth* . . . ?" he said, looking around.

"It will be a fun game for Ollie and Ella," Mom said firmly. "They can unwrap all the furniture."

Ollie loved it. He ripped all the paper off, shouting, "Weezi-weezi-weezi!"

I tried to save the paper and keep it flat so we could use it again.

"I'm just wondering," Dad said to Mom. "Is there a reason you wrapped everything in the room?"

Mom turned pink. She said, "I wanted my present to look special. Jo's presents always look special."

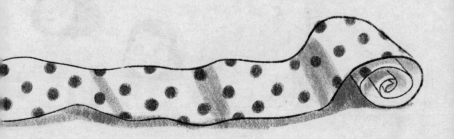

"Remember, life is not a competition," said Dad.

Then I remembered something I had once heard Mom's Fairy Tutor, Fenella, say on FairyTube. I said, " 'When fairies won't work together, magic goes wrong. When fairies work as a team, magic goes right.' "

"I know," Mom said. "You're right. It doesn't matter whose present looks better."

But she stroked the big gold pom-pom on Aunty Jo's present and looked very pleased.

* * *

That afternoon, Aunty Jo was having a birthday party at a special pottery shop. We could all go there and make something out of clay! I was very excited. Mom and Dad were there, and Aunty Jo and Granny. Ollie was there too, but he wasn't allowed to have

any clay because he would eat it, so he sat in a high chair.

We put on smocks and sat around a big table. The pottery teacher gave us lumps of clay and said we were each going to make a pot. "You're all beginners," she said. "Your pots will be simple, but they can still be beautiful."

She showed us how to make long sausages from clay and wind them around and around to make a pot. Then she said, "I will be back in half an hour," and she went out of the room.

The clay was all soft and squishy and I smooshed it with my fingers. It felt so lovely.

Then I started to roll out a sausage. Dad was rolling out his clay too. Everyone was working very quietly.

Granny was finding it difficult. She kept saying, "This wretched clay won't do what I want!"

Aunty Jo finished her pot first. It was very nice, but a little plain and a kind of lopsided. She looked at it and frowned. "Hmmm," she said. "I think this needs some help."

At once, Mom looked up from her pot, which was also a little lopsided. "Are you using magic?" she said. "Are we allowed?"

"It's my party," said Aunty Jo. "Why shouldn't we use magic?"

"I agree," said Granny, who had a smear of clay on her face and looked quite hot and bothered.

Mom, Aunty Jo and Granny all got up from their seats. They stamped their feet three times, clapped their hands, wiggled their bottoms and said "Marshmallow," "Sherbet lemon" and "Extra-strong mint," . . . and POOF! They were fairies.

"Here we go!" said Granny Fairy, looking pleased. She pointed her old-fashioned wand at her pot

and said,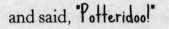

Instantly her pot turned into a wonderful vase.

"Very nice!" said Aunty Jo Fairy. She pointed at her own pot and said, "Potteridoo!" Her pot grew big and round, with a beautiful decorated edge.

"Very pretty!" Mom said. She pointed at her pot and said, "Potteridoo!" and hers turned into a lovely jug with a handle.

"Ooh," said Aunty Jo Fairy at once. "I want handles."

She pointed at her pot and said, "Handleridoo!"—and two handles appeared on her pot.

"I want handles too," said Granny Fairy. "Handleridoo! And I want a spout," she added. "Spouteridoo!"

"I want mine to be bigger," said Mom. "Biggeridoo!"

"I want *mine* to be the biggest!" said Aunty Jo Fairy. "Biggesteridoo!"

Fairy Mom, Aunty Jo Fairy and Granny Fairy all started casting lots and lots of spells. They kept shouting "Biggesteridoo!" and "Spouteridoo!" and "Handleridoo!" and waving their wands around while Dad and I stared at them.

"It's not a competition," said Dad, but no one listened.

Soon all three pots had grown up to the ceiling. They all had lots of handles and spouts and strange wiggly parts. They were the silliest, ugliest pots I had ever seen. But Fairy Mom, Granny Fairy and Aunty Jo Fairy kept doing more spells on them.

Then Aunty Jo Fairy pointed at a piece of

clay and said, "Lideridoo!" But the clay didn't turn into a lid. It started whirling around the room. Then it started spattering itself over everyone.

"Help!" said Granny Fairy as clay hit her face. "Naughty clay!"

"Weezi-weezi-weezi!" said Ollie, roaring with laughter and pointing at Granny Fairy.

Before long all the clay was flying around the room. The three pots were still growing handles and spouts. Mom had clay in her ear and Aunty Jo Fairy had clay up her nose, but they were still waving their wands and casting spells.

"This is ridiculous!" Dad shouted. "It's not a competition! Tell them, Ella!"

"'When fairies won't work together, magic goes wrong!'" I called out. "'When fairies work as a team, magic goes right.' You have to use the Teameridoo spell!"

Mom looked at me, panting, and said, "What?"

"I learned about it on FairyTube," I told her. "When you need help to work as a team, you can use the Teameridoo spell."

A piece of flying clay splatted into Mom's face and she jumped. "Ella, you're very smart," she said. "We have to work as a team or we'll *never* get the clay back under control. Jo!" she shouted. "Jo! Stop casting spells! We need Teameridoo!"

Aunty Jo Fairy looked annoyed. "It's my birthday!" she said. "I don't want to be on a team—I want to win!" But then a piece of clay whacked her on the head and she said, "Oh, I suppose you're right."

"Yes, dear," said Granny Fairy, wiping clay off her glasses. "This has gone too far. We have forgotten how to be good fairies."

Fairy Mom, Aunty Jo Fairy and Granny Fairy stood in a circle, ducking whenever the flying clay came too close. Mom and Aunty Jo Fairy pressed codes on their Computawands, and Granny Fairy waved her old-fashioned wand. Then they all said together, "Teameridoo!"

Just for a moment they all glowed, as

though a light had shone on them. They smiled at each other, and all the clay fell to the floor. The room was calmer. Everyone seemed happier.

"Phew!" Dad said. Then he heard the door open. "Uh-oh. Our teacher is coming back."

Mom looked at Aunty Jo Fairy. Aunty Jo Fairy looked at Granny Fairy. Then they all looked at each other.

"Toffee apple," said Fairy Mom.

"Blueberry pie," said Aunty Jo Fairy.

"Pancake," said Granny Fairy.

Instantly they were back to normal. Then Mom looked at the giant pots and gasped. "We didn't change the pots back!"

"Too late," Dad said as the door opened and the teacher came back in.

"Hello!" she said. "How did you do?" Then she stared at Mom in shock. "Oh dear!

You have clay all over you!"

"I was working very hard at my pot," said

Mom quickly.

Then the teacher saw the three enormous

pots. She turned quite pale and her eyes went very big. She looked at all the spouts and handles and strange wiggly parts. "Goodness," she said at last. "I've never seen pots like these in my whole life."

"Do you like mine?" said Aunty Jo. "Mine is the one with five handles and three spouts."

The teacher didn't seem able to answer. Then she saw Dad's pot. "Now, this is a beautiful pot," she said. "It is plain and simple and has been carefully made. Well done!"

Dad looked very pleased.

Aunty Jo made a sort of "hmph" noise.

"This is also a very good effort," said the

teacher, picking up my pot. "But you *all* did very well. It's not a competition," she added.

"Quite right," said Dad, and I laughed. I was remembering the clay flying around the room. I wondered what the teacher would have said if she had seen that!

* * *

After we had finished at the pottery shop, we went back to Aunty Jo's house for tea. She opened her presents and we sang "Happy Birthday" and ate a delicious cake. Then we watched Aunty Jo's favorite film, *The Sound of Fairy Music*, while I drew some pictures in my book. I drew all the strange pots, and giggled because they looked so silly. I drew the TV all wrapped up with a bow. Then I thought about working as a team. I thought that when I was a big girl and went to Fairy School, I would always work together with other fairies.

"Mom, how soon till I go to Fairy School?" I whispered.

"Not for a while yet, Ella," Mom whispered back.

"Because I can't wait to work in a fairy team."

"You already do work in a fairy team, Ella," said Mom, holding my hand tight. "And you're the best teammate ever."

CATCHERIDOO!

Stop, Thief!

My class was going on a school trip to an art gallery one day, and Mom was coming as one of the helpers. I was very excited!

As we set off for school that morning, Mom was in a good mood.

"I've worked very hard this week, Ella,"

she said, "and today I want to have fun."

It was a warm day, and Mom was wearing a beautiful dress. We drove along and the sun shone through the windows of the car and I felt so happy. I couldn't wait to get to the gallery.

Miss Amy had told us all about art galler-

ies at school. They were special places full of paintings and pictures. Some of them were by very famous artists. We would see pictures of people, pictures of different places and pictures of animals. I wondered if I might see any pictures of fairies too.

Once we arrived at school, we got on a bus. There weren't any snacks because Miss Amy said we weren't allowed snacks this time.

It didn't take long to get there. The gallery was a big building with lots of windows and a massive escalator up to the top floor. When we saw it, my best friend Tom said, "Wow!"

Then my other best friend,

Lenka, said, "I've never seen such a big escalator! It looks like a metal mountain!"

We wanted to go up and down the escalator lots more times, but Miss Amy said we had to look at the art. So we walked along to a special room, which was really big with lots of paintings on each wall. A lady was at the entrance, and as we arrived, she said, "Welcome to the *Midsummer Night's Dream* exhibition. Who would like to wear fairy wings and elf hats?"

Everyone shouted, "Me, me!"

I looked at Mom and we shared a secret smile, because the fairy wings were very small and not shiny at all. But then, they weren't real. Pretend fairies are never as good as real fairies.

I put on some fairy wings, and Lenka put on an elf hat. Tom put on fairy wings *and* an

elf hat, and we all laughed. Miss Amy put on some big fairy wings and said, "Ella, I have some fairy wings for your mom. Where has she gone?"

I looked around for her. Where *had* she gone?

Suddenly she came out from behind a door—and she was Fairy Mom! Her wings were huge and shimmery and they moved as she walked.

"I brought my own fairy wings," she said, smiling at Miss Amy.

"Goodness!" said Miss Amy, staring at Mom. "They're wonderful! And what a lovely crown!"

I couldn't believe Mom was being a fairy in front of everyone!

"Don't worry, Ella," she said quietly. "No one will guess. They think it's a costume. This is fun, isn't it?"

We all sat on the floor and the art lady talked to us about how to look at paintings.

She told us that we must all try to notice things. She said we could notice different shapes and colors. We could notice what people were doing in pictures, and what the weather was like.

Then we were allowed to walk around and look at the paintings as long as we behaved. There were other people in the gallery too, and the lady said we had to be polite and not barge into them.

Some of the paintings did have fairies in them, just like I'd hoped. Mom and I looked at a painting of a fairy sitting on a chair with a crown on her head. The painting was called *The Fairy Queen*.

"What do you notice, Ella?" Mom asked.

"I notice that the fairy is beautiful," I said. "But she looks a little sad."

"I agree," said Mom. Then she added quietly, "There's no one nearby.

Shall we see what she'd look like with a smile?"

Mom got out her phone and it turned into a Computawand. She quickly pressed a code, pointed it at the painting—*bleep-bleep-bloop*—and said, "Smileridoo!"

Suddenly the fairy in the painting was smiling, and I couldn't help giggling. She looked *much* better with a smile.

Then Mom pressed another code and said, "Normeridoo!"

The fairy was back to normal.

Then we walked on and looked at a painting with a gloomy sky.

"Let's improve the weather," said Mom.

She pressed the code, then pointed her Computawand at the painting. "Blueridoo!" she said. But instead of just the sky turning blue, the whole painting turned blue.

I gasped. "Mom! There isn't a picture anymore! There's just blue!"

"Oops!" said Mom. "I don't know how *that* happened." She quickly pressed another code and said, "Normeridoo!" and the painting went back to normal. "Maybe I'll leave the other paintings alone," she said, and I agreed with her.

She put her Computawand away just as Tom and Lenka came over.

"We've got to choose a picture and draw

it," said Tom. "I'm drawing the one of the spooky forest. Which one will you draw, Ella?"

We walked around together and looked at all the pictures, and then I saw a painting of a mermaid.

"I'm going to draw the mermaid," I said,

and smiled at Mom because we had once met real mermaids.

"Me too!" said Lenka. "I love mermaids!"

The art lady gave us pencils and pieces of paper on boards. Lenka and I sat in front of the mermaid painting and tried to copy it. I noticed that the sea was wavy and the mermaid's tail was scaly. All of a sudden, just as I was trying to copy the pattern of the scales, I heard a man yelling.

"There's been a robbery!" he was shouting.

"Someone has stolen a painting. *The Fairy Queen* has gone!"

We all gasped.

"A robber!" said Lenka. "Let's catch him!"

The next minute, a bell sounded. It was very loud, like a fire alarm.

"That means a painting has been stolen," said Mom, looking serious. "What a dreadful thing to happen."

"Don't worry!" called Miss Amy. "Everyone, stay still!"

But no one stayed still. We had all gotten up to try to catch the robber. Lenka and I were looking all around. Tom was practicing his kung fu moves.

"When we find the robber, I will do kung fu on him," he said in a fierce voice.

Tom is really good at kung fu. I thought the robber should watch out.

Suddenly we all saw a man in a black coat running to the door.

"There!" shouted Lenka. "There he is!"

She started running toward the man, but two guards in uniform had already grabbed him.

"Where is the painting?" asked one of the

guards, sounding very stern. "Do you have it?"

"No!" said the man. "I'm not the robber! I was running because I was scared of the robber!"

He took off his coat and emptied his pockets, but there wasn't a painting any-where.

"Are you hiding it in your hat?" said the other guard.

"I don't have a hat!" said the man. "I tell you, I'm not the robber!"

I looked around the gallery, and I noticed a woman in a pale coat. She was holding her hands over her coat very carefully, as though she was hiding something, and creeping toward the door.

"Mom!" I whispered. "*That's* the robber!"

Mom looked at the woman and her eyes widened. "I think you're right, Ella," she whispered back. "We need to catch her!"

Mom got out her phone and it turned into a Computawand again. She pressed a code—*bleep-bleep-bloop*—pointed it toward the woman and said, "Catcheridoo!"

But as she said it, the woman hurried quietly across the room and out of the gallery. No one else had seen her, because everyone was looking at the man and the two guards.

"I missed her!" said Mom. "She was too

quick for me! Come on, Ella—let's get her!"

We ran after the woman, but she was really fast. As we burst through the door we saw her. She was already on the escalator down, and she was nearly at the ground

floor. No one else was around to stop her.

"We'll never catch her!" I said. "She'll escape!"

"No she won't!" said Mom. She pointed her Computawand at the escalator, quickly pressed

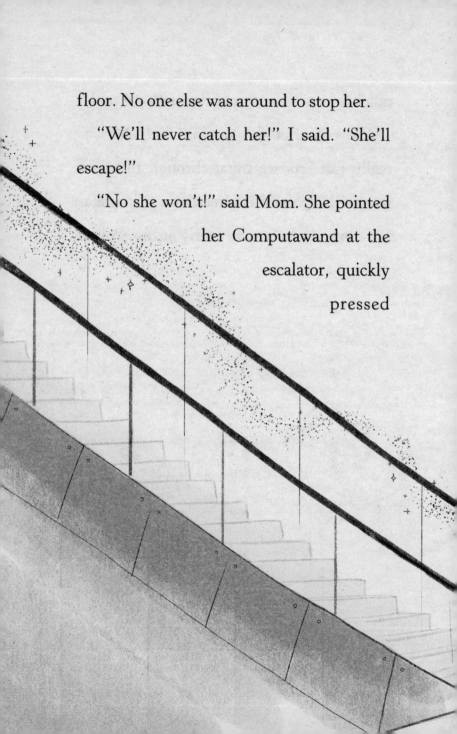

a code—*bleep-bleep-bloop*—and shouted, "Reverseridoo!"

At once the escalator changed direction. Instead of being a down escalator, it was an up escalator. It started bringing the woman toward us!

The woman looked so shocked that I started giggling.

"Stop it!" she said angrily. "I need to go down!"

"You're coming up," said Mom. "And you're giving back that painting."

The woman started trying to run down the escalator, even though it was going up.

"Oh no you don't!" said Mom. She pressed another code—*bleep-bleep-bloop*—and said, "Speederidoo!"

The escalator sped up. It whizzed the woman all the way back up to the top. She stumbled off and her coat fell open—and there was the painting of the Fairy Queen!

Mom grabbed the woman's wrist and yelled, "We've found the painting! Come quickly! Guards!"

The woman was wriggling, trying to escape, but she couldn't.

She glared angrily at Mom. "You're very

strong," she said. "Do you have special powers or something?"

"I go to the gym," said Mom, smiling.

The two guards came running over, and one grabbed the painting. "This is it!" he exclaimed. "You've caught the robber!"

The other guard was looking at the escalator in surprise.

"The escalator's broken!" he said. "It's going the wrong way. And it's too fast. We'll have to fix that."

"Yes," said Mom, winking at me. "You will. I have no idea how *that* happened."

* * *

We didn't look at any more paintings after that. The gallery was closed for the rest of the day, so we went to a café for lunch. Fairy Mom turned back into a normal mom and told Miss Amy that she had taken off her wings.

While we were all sitting at a big long table, eating our lunch, the art lady came to talk to us.

"I want to say a big thank-you to Ella and her mother for finding our painting," she said. "We are very grateful to you. Well done!"

Everyone clapped, and Tom shouted, "Hip hip hooray!"

"It was Ella who was the detective," said Mom. "She saw the woman creeping away."

"It just shows," said the art lady, "how important it is for us to use our eyes and notice things. Ella, you noticed more than anyone else in this gallery today."

As a reward she gave Mom and me each a present. It was a voucher for the gift shop. We could both choose a poster of one of the

paintings from the gallery. I was very excited. I would put the poster up in my room
and look at it every day.

"Which poster will you get?" Lenka

asked us. "Will you choose the Fairy Queen painting?"

"Yes, I think will," said Mom. "It'll remind us of our adventure. Even if she does look a little gloomy. And I think I can guess which painting Ella will choose. . . ."

"The mermaid!" I said immediately, and Mom said, "I knew it!"

And we both smiled.

FAMILY
ACTIVITY
GUIDE

TEST YOUR FAIRY
SKILLS! TURN THE
PAGE FOR LOTS OF
FUN ACTIVITIES!

BAGSERIDOO!

Design your own fairy handbag!

What do you think a fairy would keep in her handbag? Write a list here! There are a couple of ideas to start you off.

Computawand

Fairy Dust

RAINBOWERIDOO!

Make your own rainbow appear
with this fun activity. Add glitter
to make it look extra special!

* Make sure you ask a grown-up to help you cut it out.

WHAT YOU NEED:
★ A paper plate
★ Scissors
★ Paint or crayons
★ Glue (optional)
★ Cotton balls (optional)
★ Glitter (optional)

WHAT TO DO:

 1. With a grown-up's help, cut the paper plate in half. Next, cut out a semicircle from the middle of the plate, to get a rainbow shape.

 2. Use your paint or crayons to color stripes for your rainbow. Follow the curve of the plate. You can start from the top or bottom curve. Ask a grown-up to draw lines to follow, if that makes it easier.

 3. The colors of a rainbow are (starting from the top): red, orange, yellow, green, blue, purple and violet (light purple). But don't worry if you don't have all these colors. A magical rainbow can have any colors you like, in any order!

 4. If you like, you can glue cotton balls to the bottom of your rainbow, for clouds.

 5. Add glitter to your rainbow to show that it's full of rainbow magic! Next time you see a rainbow in the sky, watch out for anything unusual on your street or in your town. It might be a sign that rainbow magic is really happening. . . .

FINDERIDOO!

Can you spot these words
in the word search?

(Answers on page 149.)

APP

GLITCH

RAINBOW

SPAGHETTI

SPARKLE

SPELL BOOK

UMBRELLA

UNICORN

M	Y	D	I	F	C	Z	F	J	A	C	R
I	U	X	K	V	L	T	P	I	L	C	T
I	T	T	E	H	G	A	P	S	L	X	P
K	W	U	W	P	L	S	F	Y	E	C	W
E	O	F	N	F	I	W	L	W	R	O	W
J	W	O	A	I	T	Y	X	P	B	L	X
K	K	P	B	Y	C	V	N	N	M	Z	T
R	P	O	P	L	H	O	I	Y	U	H	J
K	D	F	O	I	L	A	R	C	I	J	L
G	S	V	Q	K	R	E	W	N	T	O	L
C	V	H	Q	O	N	C	P	T	V	A	C
S	P	A	R	K	L	E	S	S	H	W	B

WISHERIDOO!

If you had the Auto-Spell app, what would you wish for? A unicorn, like Ella does—or something else? Draw your wishes here!

ANSWERS

FINDERIDOO!

M	Y	D	I	F	C	Z	F	J	A	C	R
I	U	X	K	V	L	T	P	I	L	C	T
I	T	T	E	H	G	A	P	S	L	X	P
K	W	U	W	P	L	S	F	Y	E	C	W
E	O	F	N	F	I	W	L	W	R	O	W
J	W	O	A	I	T	Y	X	P	B	L	X
K	K	P	B	Y	C	V	N	N	M	Z	T
R	P	O	P	L	H	O	I	X	U	H	J
K	D	F	O	I	L	A	R	C	I	J	L
G	S	V	Q	K	R	E	W	N	T	O	L
C	V	H	Q	O	N	C	P	T	V	A	C
S	P	A	R	K	L	E	S	S	H	W	B

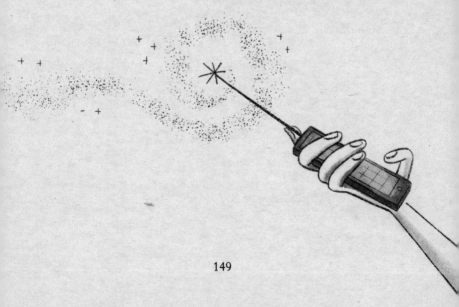

More fairy fun!